Unknowingly

Unknowingly

This is a work of fiction. Names, characters, places, and incidents are the product of the author's imagination. Any resemblance to actual organizations, events, or persons, living or dead, is entirely coincidental and beyond the intent of the author.

ISBN 978-0-578-23901-9

Printed in United States of America by 48hr Books

Acknowledgment: Abigail H. Crisostomo-Gueco, Lody D. Macatula, and Connie Macatula-De Leon

-Without them, this book would not be possible.

"Failure does not mean that it will be the end of your efforts. It does not define you. Failures are meant to be there, to be figured out in order to move on to the next step."

"Everyone has his or her own cross to carry. Even the strongest has his or her bad day. It is not how heavy or what your cross might be. Will you carry it as a burden, or will you take it as an opportunity to persevere and triumph?"

"The road to happiness has always been within us. If you cannot find it, allow somebody to help you find it."

__Author's Note__

Writing a book is a humbling and enriching experience. There is nothing quite like it. It makes you understand how small you are in this vast universe called life.

I know that I still have a long way to go as a writer, but I sincerely know that I made this book straight from the heart. The words represent how I feel, and I meant every word written in this book. I tried to write about how relationships matter especially in times of chaos and uncertainty.

Amidst the pandemic of Covid-19, I realized that what matters most are the people who we love. We should not neglect every second that we have with our family, friends, and acquaintances. These can turn into relationships of a lifetime.

Go take a chance and do something that you are passionate about. This book was made from the love of my wife, Abi, who introduced me that past tense is better than present tense. Encouraging me to do never ending revisions when I was about to give up. I can hear her laughing at the background as I write this note.

I thank my children, Nico and Marco. Without them, I will not find out how challenging it is to write amidst their unending wonder and a million questions. I am proud of them both. I hope someday when they are ready to understand what Dad has written, they will be proud of me as I am of them.

Og Mandino is my hero and I have learned a great deal from him. He is one of the reasons that inspired me to write this book. I do not know much about writing yet, but I do believe that I have a gift for storytelling. Every day I will try to strive to be a better version of myself in terms of writing, storytelling and most importantly to be a better Husband and a Dad to my sons.

I hope you find something that you are passionate about and wake up each day trying to be better at it. I hope you enjoy the story. I hope you never lose your sense of wonder.

Unknowingly

"To my dearest Abi, Nico, and Marco, never lose your sense of wonder…"

Unknowingly

Unknowingly

Unknowingly

<u>Unknowingly</u>

G.I. Gueco M.D.

May you continue to be a blessing

Unknowingly

Chapter 1
Awaits

DESMOND

I opened my eyes to a white blank wall partially lit by a dim yellow light from a streetlamp outside. "Tick, Tock, Tick, Tock!" The sound was coming from the clock above my television set.

"It's 5:20 AM." I absent-mindedly stared at the clock for two minutes and I did not want to move. I groaned and finally decided to get up.

I struggled in the darkness searching for my phone and found it underneath the pillow. I propped myself up with my elbows and sat on the edge of the bed. Rubbing my eyes with my left hand, I scrolled down my phone with my other hand to disable the alarm clock. I did not want to wake my roommates who were still fast asleep next door. I clicked the messaging app and saw no messages. As I tried to exit the room, I decided to send text messages to a friend.

"Today is D-Day! I hope you are already up. Good luck to us!"

"Good luck today! I know you will do well!"

"I will be praying for us! I will see you in school."

It was almost the end of March. *"Today is the last day of my medical school. I just took my final exams several days ago, and in a few hours, I will know the results. Today is the day that 200 medical students, including me, will know if we are going to graduate or not."*

The ceramic floor felt cold as I stepped barefoot on the common area. I shared this flat with three more friends to bring down the cost of rent. I carefully tiptoed going to the kitchen and immediately spotted the brushed stainless kettle. I turned on the stove, placed the kettle half-filled with water and poured the contents of the instant coffee sachet in my favorite mug. While I waited for the water to boil, I stood up next to the window.

Our flat was five stories up from the street. It was in an old Spanish building renovated into decent small apartments. They were a lot cheaper than most residential student facilities. It was just a stone's throw away from the university. If you looked hard enough you could see the eastside wall of the university.

"There are already some people walking in the street and I wonder if some of them are as anxious as I am, eager to know on what this day will turn out to be."

"Hmm! I wondered... How their day would turn out?"

"Hiss! Hiss!" I was startled with the sound. I almost hit my toes on the corner of the stove while I grabbed the kettle to stop it from waking my room-mates.

"Whew! Thank God! It did not wake them up! They are still fast asleep!" My roommates were nurses who worked the unholy 2 PM-10 PM shifts. They were late sleepers and were probably right in the middle of their deep slumber.

I poured the hot water in my mug. It was still dark outside, and streetlights were still on. I saw the window silhouette on the floor created by the light outside as it struck my window. I stood still in the darkness enjoying a moment of silence while I smelled the strong aroma of hot coffee mixed with the sweet breeze coming from the open window.

As I sipped the last drop of my coffee, I headed towards my dresser and took out my last white uniform which I just washed and ironed last night.

I stood in front of the mirror and saw my re-flection. I'm 5'11" but a lot of people said I looked taller than my height. Maybe because of my wide and broad shoulders. My jet-black hair was already getting long, and I badly needed a haircut. My deep-seated eyes framed with long eyelashes were what my mom doted a lot. But right now, I saw the weight of what the long sleepless nights of studying has done to my eyes.

"Thankfully, that is all done now. I still have short stubbles along my squared jawline which I plan to shave depending on what today's outcome will be."

I pinned my green name plate on my uniform and closed the door behind me as I walked out into the hallway. It was still empty and quiet. I could clearly hear my footsteps echoing as I went down the stairs.

"Good morning, Sir!" Greeted the guard down in the lobby.

"Good morning!" I responded to the new guard whom I just saw for the first time.

I usually say, "Hi" to Arnold every morning. He was the previous guard whom I befriended. But I could not do that anymore as he died in his sleep two nights ago for reasons unknown. He died in the sleeping quarters underneath the stairs.

I could see the old folding bed where he used to sleep as I was about to step out into the sidewalk. I silently offered a prayer for him. I wish I were there to help him.

The street where I lived was barely 50 yards away from the gate of the university. I chose the place to avoid the hassles of traffic. With just a few steps, I could be in the medical school building in no time.

Walking towards the eastside gate, I saw the street vendors fixed their tents and makeshift food shops that lined the sidewalk. I headed straight to the middle-aged lady who was opening a huge patio umbrella and helped her. Even though it was still early in the morning, she was getting ready to set it up to protect her customers once the sun comes out.

"Good morning Josie! Are you already open?"

"You betcha I am, Desmond," she brightly replied. "Are you going to have the usual?"

"How did you know it's me Josie?"

"You are always on time. Same time, different day!" Josie replied with a silly smile on her face.

"Of course, the usual! You really know me that well," I grinned at her. I sat in one of the monobloc white chairs and delightedly ate the warm rice porridge with green onions, hard-boiled egg, and a few drops of lemon juice.

Most of the vendors here were my friends. I often talk to them before and after school. They sort of became my family. But Josie was one of my favorites. She was like a long-lost Aunt. As I finished my meal, I stood up and paid for my hearty breakfast.

"Good luck today, Desmond! I know you will pass!" She happily exclaimed.

"Look at you, looking sharp! You remembered."

"I can be as old as one of your aunts, but I am not that too old, Desmond!" Josie giggled.

"I hope you are right, Josie. Thank you and I will see you later." I gave her a high five which brought a huge grin on her face.

A group of students are gathered near the crossing light. I tried to hurry up as I saw the "Walk" sign flashing. Jeepneys and cars were already moving from one end to the other. They seemed to forget traffic rules as they stopped in the middle of the road dropping students off near the gate.

I could see the huge black gates that were now wide open, which gave one a full view of the front of the university library. On my left, I saw the friendly candy vendor who was flashing a wide smile at me. Her eyes were fixed at me as she waited for me to pass by her stall.

"How are you handsome?"

"I am good. How about you beautiful?"

Nene giggled. "I'm good! I'm good!"

She reached towards her candy stash and handed me a couple of candies and said, "Good luck Desmond! I know you'll make it. Do not forget about us."

"You know that I won't!"

"Thank you, Nene." I gave her a fist bump and headed towards the medical school building.

As usual, I admired the picturesque century-old acacia trees that surrounded it. In front of the building was the "Rod of Asclepius" symbol, with Latin words around it. I was surprised that a lot of students were gathered in front of its gate.

It was just half-hour past seven. I decided to go to my favorite bench underneath the acacia trees. I saw my classmates, friends, and other acquaintances, who like me, were eagerly waiting for this day.

Most of the 200 students were already gathered around the pavilion. I sensed the air of excitement and anxiety around me. I felt the butterflies in my stomach as I waited for all of us to get inside the building and know the results. At exactly 8:00 AM, the list would be posted. We would know the ones who passed and unfortunately, the students who would need to repeat the whole year all over again.

"Hey, Des! Are you ready for this? I feel nauseated, I feel like I'm going to throw up!" A classmate tried to start a small talk with me while biting her fingernails and unconsciously tapping her feet on the cement floor like a nervous tic. I thought she did it to relieve her anxiety.

"No, I am not! Nobody will be ready for this! I feel nervous too, but I think we will make it, especially you!" I smiled at her and tried to reassure her.

"Yeah, right!" She then stopped biting her nails and flashed a grin at me. Her nervousness eased after she talked to me.

"You know what, I think the guards are already allowing the students to go inside. We better head to the second floor for the announcement," she said excitedly.

As I walked inside the building with the rest of the students, I begin to ponder on the importance of this day.

I cannot count the sleepless nights, missed meals, and sacrifices I had endured for this moment. A mere piece of white paper will determine my future today.

A petite woman in a blue suit precipitously appeared carrying a list of names who passed with honors. She posted it and left quickly, trying to avoid the students who flocked eagerly in front of the bulletin board. The names listed were no longer a surprise. They were undeniably the brightest and most deserving!

I saw a group gathered around a student and everyone was trying to shake her hand.

"Who is that?" I asked a fellow student who was next to me.

"She is our *summa cum laude*!"

"Awesome!"

The crowd soon thinned out and I went to see for myself who was in the list and looked for any further announcements that they posted.

"…exam results are still being deliberated upon and we will announce them today as soon as they are finalized!"

"Pft!" I groaned in frustration. I cannot believe I had to wait this long. I looked at the list again and saw a familiar name.

"Clarice H. Landere!"

Seeing her name made me smile from ear to ear. Suddenly, I smelled a familiar fresh crisp scent and felt a hand on my shoulder. Even without turning around, I knew it was her. I intuitively gazed at her adoringly. She had long dark brown hair tied in a neat ponytail with a black scunci. Her dazzling sapphire eyes were captivating and could melt any guy's heart. Her smile was stunning, but her eyes looked tired and worried.

"I was just thinking about you and suddenly, here you are!" I said excitedly.

"Hi Des! How are you holding up with all this nonsense waiting?" Clarice asked me with a worried look on her face.

I flashed a grin at her and said, "Don't worry about me. You know, they usually make the gorgeous students wait. I bet you, my name will be first on that list when they release it shortly."

Clarice shook her head in disbelief. She chuckled and pinched my cheeks playfully. I smiled at her. It had been a habit of her to pinch my cheeks every time I make her laugh. I do not know why, but I feel good every time she does that. I always want to make her happy.

"I'll be alright!" I said. "By the way, I saw your name on the list. Your hard work paid off! I am so proud of you. You did one hell of a job, Ms. *magna cum laude!*"

"Thank you, Des! That's so sweet of you. But still, I am worried about you. How I wish they release the results soon." She leaned towards me and patted my right shoulder.

My worries melted like butter as soon as she did that. I then tried to reassure her and said, "Don't worry, when I get the results, I'll let you know at once and we will celebrate!"

Out of nowhere, we suddenly heard a lot of voices yelling her name excitedly.

"Clarice! Clarice! Clarice! You did it!" All her friends flocked at her and were squealing while they congratulated her. They screamed and shrieked happily while doing celebratory jumps around her.

Feeling left out, I moved aside. Her eyes are now slit-like as her grin got wider from ear to ear. She really looks cute whenever her eyes disappeared like that. Her cheeks are flushed and reddish. She looked embarrassed with all the attention she was getting. Our eyes met and I nodded at her. I waved goodbye and headed my own way.

Unknowingly

Chapter 2
Clarice

CLARICE

As I was surrounded by my friends, I saw Desmond waved goodbye to me. He did not want to spoil my moment. He stepped aside and let me enjoy it with my friends. He had a worried look in his eyes but still pretended everything was OK. I said a silent prayer and I hoped he passes. He walked downstairs and slowly disappeared from my view.

I had known Desmond for several years, it all started after a chance meeting we had. We had always been there for each other. I saw him at his happiest and at his most trying times. I had been a shoulder to cry on when his heart was broken by failed relationships.

I had been there for him during moments of unexplained sadness, the reasons for which he would not disclose. Despite all these difficulties, he would continue to bounce back like a champ. He was one of the most stubborn individuals I knew but despite that, he was still able to endear himself to people. He was gutsy and unrelenting.

"Stoikiy muzhik," which meant standing man as Rudolf Abel from the movie "Bridge of Spies" would say. Desmond would continue to stand up no matter what the odds may be.

I let out a deep sigh. *"How I wish I can talk to him right now. I should be ecstatic that I will graduate magna cum laude, but none of that makes me feel good and happy.*

"Today is my mother's death anniversary. I loved my mom and I missed her so much. I wished she could see me right now - on what I became, on what I have accomplished. At 24 years old, I cannot believe I made it this far. I will be graduating

magna cum laude with a Medical Degree. I would give up anything just to have her here by my side."

I have two loving friends, Carla and Chaisse. We had been close friends since our pre-med days in Biology. Their faces were all lit up as they shrieked with delight. They could not contain their excitement as they danced around me while screaming wildly! "We will all graduate with honors!"

"Yes! We did it! More power to the Triple C beauties!" Carla exclaimed.

"Triple C beauties: Clarice, Carla and Chaisse. I like that!" Chaisse affirmed Carla's moniker for our group! "We need to celebrate," she said to both of us.

"Oh...You guys are too much! But yes, we'll do that! Let's celebrate and hang out in our favorite dinner club, the Curb! My treat!" I said to both as I tried to keep up with their bliss.

"Yeah! Great idea!" Chaisse agreed.

"No! It's going to be my treat! I'll call later and set it up for this coming Friday. I'll reserve the whole club. Let's invite our friends." Carla giggled excitedly.

"Thanks Carla! But you don't have to," I said to her.

"No, I insist. That is the least I can do for you, Guys! It's settled. My treat!" She said happily.

"Alright, Carla! Whatever you say! Thanks, my friend. Triple C! Triple C! Triple C! Triple Threat in the house!" Chaisse shouted crazily without a care in the world as we went down to exit the medical building.

I giggled and celebrated with my friends, but what I felt inside was totally a different story. Deep within me, I am suffering from a secret desperation and sorrow that I kept hidden from everyone else.

Unknowingly

"Why am I not happy?" I silently asked my-self.

"Everybody will think how lucky I am! I have a dozen of Christian Louboutin shoes, a wide collection of Hermes bags and now, the 2nd highest honor in medical school, magna cum laude! But still, there is this hollow feeling inside me. I feel so empty.

"Do not get me wrong. I am grateful with everything I have. I do not take anything for granted. I know how fleeting the joy of these material things brought me and I tried my best to cherish them. But still, I feel incomplete.

"I feel like a 1,000-piece puzzle missing a piece to make it whole. No matter how awesome it is, it will never be complete as it was lacking something. All these years, I got better in hiding my sorrows. I got better in pretending and keeping my sadness at bay.

"Mom, I am getting tired of this feeling. Each year, it gets harder without you, Mom." I silently said to myself.

"I wish I can talk to you, Mom. If you were here, things will be different." But this would have to do for now. I knew I needed to be strong. I kept a happy face even though it was not how I felt inside.

I spent the rest of the morning chit-chatting with my friends. Then, they left one by one as they went on their own ways. Finally, it was just Carla and me who were left in the pavilion.

"Clarice, do you want to come and hang out with me at home?" Carla asked as her chauffeur drove by to pick her up.

"No, thank you. I'll be fine. I also have plans to meet up with my dad. You go ahead, I'll just see you later." I hugged her and said goodbye.

"I'll call you later, bye!"

Unknowingly

As my friend's car disappeared from my view, I felt all alone. My mind was blank. I started to walk away from the building without knowing where I was headed.

Unknowingly

Chapter 3
Remembering

DESMOND

I went outside the medical school building and reached the covered walkway. I saw a lot of students still gathered inside the big pavilion. I stopped and wondered what I would be doing while I waited.

I began to walk without a destination in mind. As I strolled aimlessly, I started to appreciate the buildings with their Spanish-architectural designs and the green lush open fields around me. This university was old. It had been around for more than 100 years. A lot of people had walked the same path I was taking, walked the same hallways I had been. This university had been a witness to all the great stories ever told.

But today is my story. In a few hours, I will know how it begins. I passed by the high school building adjacent to a little-known passage near the church. It had been a while since I came here. I opened the huge chain-linked gate and went inside.

I knew my parents were waiting for my call, but I decided to delay calling them. A lot had happened leading to this day. I would not have made it if they did not teach me wisely. I have always learned from them that the rewards are greater once I surpass the obstacles ahead of me.

I love my parents dearly and their voices of wisdom guide me in my daily struggles. I could still remember my dad telling me to always remember three most important things…INTEGRITY, COURAGE, and GRIT.

"What do they mean, Dad?" A younger me asked curiously.

"Do you remember the time a customer asked me to fix his radio and I didn't find anything wrong except for a stuck power button? I could have asked him to pay for my services but instead, I did not charge him. Doing the right thing when no one is looking is called Integrity!"

"OK, Dad. How about courage and grit?" I asked again.

"Remember the time when our neighbor's house caught on fire? For a minute, everybody stood still while "Granny" was screaming for help. Everyone, including me, was frightened to dash through the fire and save her. I soaked a blanket and together with her son, we got her out. You will always have fears. Courage happens when you are able to do things despite your fears."

"The last is grit! We have not always struggled for money. We had a booming business once, but as fate would have it, some good things don't last forever. We sold everything including my favorite possession, my pick-up truck! Your mom and I did not give up even if it meant for us to touch bottom. We would do that again if we had to, just to make sure that you and your siblings finished school."

"Thanks Dad! I promise to remember them!"

Now, I reached a cross path. I wandered around the botanical garden and came across an alternative, seldom-used path. Behind some trees, I saw timeworn wood benches that people would often use to hear mass. I heard church songs being sang by the choir. I found myself seated on one of the benches. From where I sat, I saw the altar. I felt the calming sound of their voices and felt a warm pressure on my chest. This was the very same feeling that I had when I encountered something that touched me unexpectedly.

"…hide me in thy wounds. That I may never leave thy side. From all the evil that surrounds me, defend me. And when the call of death arrives. Bid me come to thee. That I may praise thee with thy saints forever."

I found myself singing along with the choir. I have sung that song to myself many times before. I often sang it to comfort myself when I was faced with a difficult situation. I knelt and said a little prayer.

"No matter what the results may be, please help me accept it. Let your will be done."

I stood up and started walking on the paved road connecting the university church to the open field. I thought of my parents as I walked.

My father is a stunning huge man. He could grasp someone's skull with one hand. He boasted of unending stories. One story involved a fight started by his friends. He tried to break it up but ended up in it. Towards the end, he was left alone and cornered. His friends ran away and unintentionally left him behind. Knowing he was alone, he grabbed one of the guys who was near him, locked his head up underneath his arm and said to the group in a loud confident voice.

"Do your worse!"

The fight was broken up by the police eventually, but the courage displayed by my dad earned the respect of his peers.

He told that story to me to make a point.

"When somebody or something tries to knock you down, keep trying to stand up no matter how hard it might be. Your perseverance will pay off in the end."

My father loved me unconditionally. He was as gentle and caring as you would like a father to be to his son. He placed me first before anything else. He would even give the food in his hand to satisfy my hunger before his.

He had struggled for us. He never complained. I saw him carrying 5-gallon containers to schools and hospitals up a flight of stairs with no elevators. There was one time he fell which left a scar on his face. He woke up every single day doing the same thing to support his family. In a few hours, he will see the result of his grit through me.

I was deep in my thoughts. I did not realize that I wandered into this garden, where I usually go to find peace and to get away from what was bothering me at the moment. It was my refuge when I wanted to feel safe and secured. That feeling reminded me of my mother.

I remembered her understanding and patience. The one instance that stuck with me throughout the years was when I was 17 years old. I slipped out of the house to have a drink with my friends without asking permission. I came home at two in the morning. I thought she would be upset and disappointed. Instead of going home to a furious mother, there was a fresh dinner waiting for me.

"I noticed you have not eaten before you left. After eating, you go get some rest." I would never forget my mother's kindness.

I was almost at the end of the narrow path that led to the open field where Pope John Paul II was greeted by thousands of students when he visited our university a few years ago. Everyone was delighted and felt blessed that day.

I saw the open field now. It was surrounded by Victorian cast iron garden benches filled with visitors and students. It was almost close to nine in the morning. I saw students in their yellow shirts and black shorts engaged in football practice throughout the open field. I saw this huge open space filled with freshly cut green grass. Weirdly, the smell of freshly cut green grass stimulated my senses and somehow, I felt bliss.

The open field was surrounded with students seated on the benches. They were waiting for their turn to practice. I saw a familiar face in a white physician coat, mingling with the students. He's my friend and one of my mentors, Dr. Doble. I waved at him and he motioned me to talk to him as if like a father who had not seen his son for a long time.

Dr. Florentino C. Doble is one of the best surgeons in the country. He did not talk much, giving the impression that he was unapproachable. But once you get to know him very well, you will find him to be one of the most authentic, respected, and humble physicians around.

With his deep low voice, he asked, "What are you doing here? Aren't you supposed to be reading right now and studying?"

"Today is D-Day when I will know if I pass or not."

"And you came to church, asking God to spare you and let you pass." He said this with a smile as he stood up and hugged me.

"You will be fine!"

He got a message from his beeper requesting him to go back to the hospital. He wished me good luck!

Everyone in the field was pretty much preoccupied. Students practiced drills and coaches directed them from end to end. This was a favorite place for runners. Most of the medical students, professors and physicians woke up early to jog around in this field. I usually spend around 45 minutes, four times a week jogging or brisk walking in this place with my friends and classmates.

The field also had gazebos where some students stayed in between classes. Unlike the library, silence is not imposed here. That's why one would often hear teasing, laughter, and even soft music from cellphones or other small electronic gadgets.

As I walked around the rectangular field, I saw friends talking to each other. They enjoyed each other's company. But sometimes I saw people seated alone eating by themselves, with their heads down.

I remembered my conversation with my friend Arnold before he died. We talked a few weekends ago when he was done with his criminal justice final exam. Arnold was a working student. He was the guard I befriended. Around wooden chairs, a makeshift table and some iced-cold beers, Arnold opened up about his loneliness.

"To the lucky few, someone will be there when they need them the most. But for some, they will spend their time with loneliness with no one to turn to and share their problems with.

"Some had been masters of hiding their bitterness and loneliness. Their feeling of emptiness and neglect is unrecognized even by the very people who have the capacity to help them get out of the hole they unwittingly made for themselves." Arnold had a slight slur in his speech. He grabbed his beer and took another sip.

"You are right!" I exclaimed as I agreed with Arnold. "Loneliness is the most denied feeling or state of mind that one tends to suppress or keep for herself or himself. Talking about it, gives a sense of discomfort. Suppressing it instead of sharing it is often the way most will deal with it."

"It leads to a plethora of troublesome feelings and state of mind. It creeps on you like an unwanted burglar, taking all that it wants. If you allow it, it takes away your sense of joy, excitement, and your will. You do not even realize what it is taking away from you."

Arnold reached into his pocket and brought out a box of reds. He lit one and turned his head away from me as he exhaled his smoke out and continued talking.

"It isolates you. It fools you into believing that you do not have a purpose. It does not even force you to feel that way. It just waits for you to unknowingly allow it in your life. Loneliness is more than a state of being physically alone. It is a state where you allow your life to be filled with no sense of purpose and emptiness even if you are the richest and most beautiful person in the room."

Surprisingly, he made sense as I listened to him while I sipped my beer.

"It does not pick skin color, race, culture, age or gender. There is no laboratory test that can detect it. Nor is there any one way of dealing with it. True is the statement that no one knows how it starts. What events and circumstances allow it to grow in one's self without letting the person know he or she has it? It hits you like a truck. It is like an accident that you could never predict, when and how it will happen.

"You will have moments that you think you already figured things out. But to your surprise, tears come rolling down your cheek leading you to a darker state of loneliness, depression."

I nodded in agreement with him, I pointed to the magazine beside him as I shared my position on the matter at hand.

"You read the news of famous people, going into this dark side of loneliness. You begin to wonder why they succumb to it despite being so successful. They have all the money and fame. But still you will hear stories of them dying due to unrecognized loneliness despite being surrounded by loved ones.

"It is like the wind that nobody sees or touch, but you know it is there. Is this the reason why people who are lonely somehow appear on surface that they have already managed to deal with their loneliness only to succumb to it in the end? They let their guard down, not knowing it is still there."

Arnold answered quickly while gesturing with his hands in the air.

"What about people with unfavorable circumstances or abuses? They had learned how to suppress it. It resurfaces and consumes everything they had desperately worked hard for in dealing with it. There is no magic pill that can extinguish it. It is like a fire that starts small and just give it a chance, it will spread like wildfire." I now see that Arnold had twice the beer that I had but to my surprise, his mind appears to be as razor-sharp as ever. He continued.

"What is the point if it is a pervasive feeling that nobody can shake and get rid of? It demands from anyone who has it the respect it deserves. It needs to be recognized and brought to the surface instead of staying hidden forever."

I found myself seated alone on one of the benches covered by pine trees. There was a slight wind coming from the east, which made the field cooler than usual. I could smell the distinctive piney scent emitted by trees that shaded the sides of the field. This university pretty much became my second home. Thousands of bus trips, miles and hours spent in trying to survive the rigors of nine years of higher-level education, which culminated on today's event - the much-awaited release of our final test results.

Basically, this was the place where I matured and transitioned in becoming an independent and responsible adult.

One thing was for certain, I did not neglect relationships, even if they were as simple as an acquaintance or a passing moment. I learned from my dad how to appreciate whoever is in front of me.

"Do not forget the importance of small talk," as my dad would say.

My dad taught me to treat everybody, from the janitor to the CEO of a company, as I would treat my family. My father emphasized relationships start with small talk. He told me not to underestimate the power hidden behind it. There are no rules with small talk. Just do it spontaneously and see where it will lead you.

I remembered my on-call nights in the hospital. I would see the same security guard as I left early in the morning. One of those mornings, I went to the coffee vending machine and got two cups of coffee. I carefully carried this through the halls and down the steps. Finally, I reached the entrance of the hospital.

"Good morning, Sir! Care for a cup of coffee?" I recalled saying to the guard.

I talked to him and asked if he just started his shift, how he was and even asked how his family was doing? I saw from his eyes, the sense of self-worth. The sense of being seen.

That day marked the beginning of a beautiful friendship. Every time he sees me, he will greet me and ask how I am doing. We became good friends.

This was true the other way around. Whenever I talked to someone important, a person of title and position, I talked to them with the same personable and sincere way. The feeling they got was the same. Feeling seen and recognized.

I realized starting a small talk did not require education or formal training. It just needed to be authentic and sincere. It did not need to be patronizing or any exaggeration. My words were always heartfelt and sincere. Sincerity opened doors. It provided comfort to those who were restless and calmed the most untrusting individuals.

I smiled as I recalled these events. I watched people walked by, without them acknowledging that I was there too. They were either engrossed in their conversation with the person that they were walking with or were thinking of something else.

I got up again and went for a walk around the open field. I had done this a thousand times during my stay here in this university. I started as an RN (Registered Nurse) and eventually pursued a medical degree. I loved the thought of becoming a nurse first before going to medical school. It gave me a different, more relevant perspective. I knew Nursing would make me a better physician.

Before I knew it, the field was now filled with students who were taking their breaks. As I glanced around me, I noticed a familiar face.

I saw Clarice seated alone on a bench. I wondered what she was still doing here since she already knew that she was graduating, with *magna cum laude* honors to boot.

"How are you my Clarice?" Clarice was surprised to see me.

"I am OK, I guess. I'm just passing time," responded Clarice with a worried look on her face.

"There was an announcement by the student body council. The deliberation of remaining students who passed and failed will be finished by around 3 PM." Clarice remarked.

I learned that there was a problem in calculating the scores in the surgery department. Dr. Mendez, the medical professor, who taught it, failed 80% of the students. This meant, 80% of the entire batch had to repeat a year of remedial.

The student council deliberated with the faculty. They tried to defend the 80% of batch from failing. Grades were being recomputed and the final exam was being reevaluated. To validate the reasonableness of the test prepared by Dr. Mendez, a dozen practicing MD's (senior attending physicians and medical residents) were requested to take a simulated test using the material prepared by Dr. Mendez. As expected, most of the "examinees" plunked the test. Thus, the valid argument that the final test was not a true or reasonable measure of grading the medical students who took the recent surgery test.

There had been talks and rumors that the whole final surgery exam will be scrapped and considered as void. If this held true, more would be passing and would not need to repeat a whole year of medical school.

I was ecstatic to see Clarice. I sat down to her right.

"Did you tell your family yet of you graduating with honors?"

"No, not yet!"

"I held off in calling my parents too until the results come in. What are you still doing here?"

"My father is running late, and I am waiting to meet up with him as he promised several days ago. As usual, he was caught in an important meeting that went past its scheduled time. I found myself sitting here to while away the time."

I slightly nodded my head in agreement and then asked her if I could wait with her. Clarice agreed and our conversation started.

Unknowingly

Chapter 4
Small Talk

DESMOND

Benches around the field were filled with students. It was midday and was easy to miss that Clarice and I were amidst the crowd. I felt the wind as it swayed the leaves and tiny branches like dancing to music. You could hear the incomprehensible words that rang out from students who chatted among themselves. My own conversation with Clarice was drowned in the midst of the crowd.

Clarice looked young for her age. She preferred a dark blue frame with her glasses to complement her eyes. Her clothes were nicely ironed with a smell of fresh lavender. Her shoes and handbag matched the billboard displayed in malls and television commercials with celebrities who wore them. She had a certain elegance to her and demeanor that would tell you that she was reserved and controlled in the way she interacted with people. I got closer to her, to hear what she was about to say.

"My father asked me to wait while he tries to finish a board meeting." I noticed her dreary face as she gazed at me momentarily before she looked down as if trying to avoid eye contact.

"Do you feel alright?"

"I did not have enough sleep the past few nights and I've been feeling tired lately. Otherwise, I am alright."

Clarice lived by herself in her own apartment with a driver and a maid to help with daily things. Her father, Mr. Landere, was the only relative she had in the country. Most of her relatives were abroad. She was an only child.

Mr. Landere was the Chief Executive Officer of a major brewing and food company. I hardly met him. I saw him once with Clarice and when he was around, he does not say much. He was a tall 6-foot-5-inch man with an imposing figure. He had broad shoulders and an aloof demeanor.

Clarice seemed to be quiet. She was not talking like she normally did.

"How is everything at home?" I tried to engage her.

"Everyone was sent home for a break. It will be just me and dad later." She did not look forward to going home.

Clarice's mother, Diana, died when she was young. She avoided talking about her mother. The only thing I knew about her was that she died when Clarice was eight years old.

It was different when her mother was alive. Her family often went in and out of the country with frequent visits to Disneyland. After Diana died, Mr Landere buried himself with work. He left Clarice mostly with household help and her driver. He became distant and inaccessible. Clarice grew up mostly alone and with the memory of her once happy family.

Unknown to me, Clarice thought about her mother, Diana. Her death anniversary was today.

I did not know much about her death. I saw Clarice silent as she stared at the sky. I did not want to bother her. She was in deep thought. I let her be silent for a while. I know she will talk when she is ready.

Suddenly, there was a flashback that filled Clarice's memory. It was a sunny beautiful Monday afternoon when she found her not responding to her yells and pleads. She found her mother hanging with a self-made noose in her walk-in closet.

Diana suffered from depression. Like people with this ailment, she had lost pleasure in doing things. She felt alone and helpless. She went into a deep hole of unexpected and undesirable state of sadness. Her depression got worse after giving birth to Clarice. She stopped going out and most of the time she just read self-help books at home.

It was difficult for an eight-year-old Clarice to process such a vision of her mother, lifeless in front of her. She went through with it alone amidst several sessions of cognitive behavioral therapy with her therapist. Her father dealt with his own sadness and chose work as a means of escape.

Without her therapist, she would have not finished high school and college. Mr. Landere often would not go home for days. He would avoid home because it reminded him of her. He unknowingly left Clarice on her own. He turned to his work and alcohol as his coping mechanism.

"Today is her death anniversary."

It had been harder for Clarice to cope and get through this difficult day each year. Her sadness and depression got worse as this day approached. In the past, she was even admitted in an inpatient psychiatric unit because of her uncontrolled depression with suicidal ideation.

With no one to turn to, not even her dad, she battled with it everyday alone. She had done well in keeping this to herself. She did not trust anyone, and felt it was a cross that she alone should carry.

Clarice suppressed her feelings and blamed herself. She thought of sharing it with others but was afraid of being perceived as weak. She denied her feelings until her body forced her to pay attention to it.

She felt her depression kept her in a deep hole where the light does not touch the bottom. Sometimes, she felt that she was beyond help. She did not even know when to ask for help.

Clarice knew that some people around her had their own problems, too. It was part of human nature to at least think of others when they needed help. Most would ignore it and move on. One cannot blame others because they battled their own darkness and weaknesses. It was also a choice to stop, listen, and be a part of the answer that others might need, and most were praying for.

To be fair, Clarice did not fully understand why some would stop and gave their own time to help others. They are not obligated to do so and yet they shared themselves to prove that every person was a part of a link. A link that one should choose to be a part of. You need to reach out for the link to work. One part must be attached to the other, or else everything would fall and crumble.

Clarice glanced at me quickly as if I were not there. She was preoccupied with her thoughts and something was bothering her. I decided to break my silence and engaged her into a little conversation.

"I am worried about the results. What if I fail? How will I tell my parents? I have not called them yet. I failed once. I saw how affected my mother and father were. They have gambled everything they have for me to finish my medical education."

Clarice smiled and replied, "I have seen how you studied. You have given more effort than most students that I know. I am pretty sure that whatever the results may be, they would reflect on how hard you have worked for this. Giving it your all, would give you a sense of having no regrets whatever the outcome may be."

"True!"

I dreaded to call my parents. I had not returned their call yet since this morning. I had been familiar with failure. If not because of my dad, I would have a different way of dealing with it. I could have given up a long time ago. A lesson my Dad taught me was to welcome failure.

"Failure does not mean that it will be the end of your efforts. It does not define you. Failures are meant to be there, to be figured out in order to move on to the next step."

If I made a mistake, my dad taught me to welcome it and embrace it. If it made me feel sad,

let it make me feel sad and upset. Let your disap-
pointment show but put a timeframe on how long it
was supposed to linger in your mind. Do not let it
stay with you forever.

I said to myself, "I will be sad for two days
then I'll worry about something else. Or better yet, I
will worry about how to do better next time in order
not to commit the same mistake."

I looked at Clarice and as our eyes met, I
proudly declared, "Come to think of it, I agree! I
gave it my all. Whatever the results may be, I will be
OK with it. But I still feel anxious and scared! " I
winked at Clarice with a grin.

"Have you decided yet on what to do after
this Clarice? I know you will be a great doctor."

"I do not know yet, but I'll think about it when
the time comes." Clarice stroked the side of her
face as she replied.

She turned to me and smiled. "I think you can become a good psychiatrist if you choose to be."

"Is it because of my winning personality?" I teased her and for the first time, I saw her laughed.

"There is the laugh that I was looking for. I hope whatever you are feeling will get better. I, too, have those days at times. I am glad I am here with you."

Clarice anxiously thought of telling me what today means for her. She felt unexpectedly at ease by this time.

"Desmond...Today is the day when my mom died. I have been thinking about her the whole day. I miss her and it has been harder each year to handle the sadness of this day."

I felt a sudden gush of shock and surprise. I did not realize how difficult this day was for Clarice.

She probably was having a roller coaster of emotions that she would not be able to relay into words.

I struggled to keep calm and tried hard to present a tough facade, "What you just did is absolutely hard. Thank you for sharing the significance of this day. I am glad that I am with you." I reached out and held her trembling hands. For a couple of minutes nothing was spoken. Clarice and I remained silent.

"Listening and being silent when one had an opinion with everything, or anything was hard to do. I often wondered, if everyone wanted to share their thoughts, how many would be left to listen?"

Clarice felt a warm calming pause as I acknowledged how difficult the day was for her. She felt the wall of pressure caving in on her has stopped. The loneliness that she had been enduring, suddenly became bearable and ceased crushing her inside.

Clarice started to regain her composure. Her nerves had gently calmed down. "My father had been coping with it differently. After my mother died, he spent most of his time with his company. He seldom goes home and stays away from things that would remind him of her."

Mr. Landere had forgotten everyone including himself and his daughter. If he was not working, he would be away drinking. He had unintentionally forgotten that he had a daughter who needed him. He still loved her daughter, but she had been buried beneath the overwhelming sorrow that he was trying to get rid of. He had put her aside. Everyday, he tried to deal with his grief. The deeper the hole of despair he made for himself, the larger the emotional gap he created between him and his daughter.

Clarice tried to live each day without her mother and dealt with an emotionally unavailable father as best as she could. There were days she managed it well and there were days, like today, when the pressure is just overwhelming. She felt like the sky was crushing down on her.

Despite how much she had gone through, today she graduates with honors. She had been stronger than most who could have easily given up. But even the strong had days of sadness, which can eventually overpower them.

"It is like a constant drop of water on a solid rock. Give it time and it would pierce through the hard rock and create a hole of emptiness. It just took time for it to destroy anything on its path. Unlike the rock that does not have a choice, a person had the option to stay stagnant like the rock or figure out a way to get away from the emptiness." Clarice thought to herself.

Clarice continued, "I dread going home today! I will be alone. No one to talk to. I decided to stay here at least for the time being. I know I told you that my dad will meet up with me. But I know that he will not. He is probably feeling the same way as I do and probably even worse. I saw the open field and the students gathering around. Being here is a better option.

"I am glad that by chance you saw me and was willing to pass the time with me. Thank you for listening to me Desmond! Sharing one's thoughts and feelings with someone who is non-judgmental and empathetic indeed helps a lot. Thank you for being you and for being authentic."

I did not know how to respond to that. I was somewhat embarrassed. I thought that her gratitude was a bit too much for what I have done to her. I leaned over to embrace her tight!

"You are welcome, Clarice!"

"I am really sorry that I am a hugger. I did not intend to do that. I felt giving you one. I am not sure how I helped but I think me being gorgeous helps!" I attempted to hide my feeling of awkwardness by way of my half-baked apology and funny quote. Clarice must have noticed that I blushed.

Clarice gave me a raised eyebrow and pretended to look annoyed. After a second, we both began to laugh again.

Clarice's cellphone rang. It was Mr. Landere. She excused herself and stood up to talk to him. I made a hand gesture for her to go ahead. She took the call.

It was twelve-minutes past noon. Most students were passing through to get to lunch. I did not have the urge to eat at this point. I was too worried about the results.

I decided to call my parents to give them an update and I reassured them of my expectations. By this time, I thought that they would be worried about me. My father's health had been frail lately. His body had taken a toll. He recently was diagnosed with a stroke and he was dependent on others to care for him. Though I saw him struggled at times, I knew that he had more left in him. He had always tried to live his life as a good man, and he had been a good father to me.

I observed the kindness of my parents many times. I remembered seeing my father unexpectedly in my doorsteps during times I did not come home to study for an exam. He would ask me to take a break and watch a movie with him. We would hurry up, early in the morning, to catch the early showing of a movie. Those moments may be simple to many, but they meant a lot me.

I remembered when my mother slipped some extra money in my bag. I never let her know that I struggled to pay rent, books, uniforms, and even my meals for the day. I resorted to doing odd jobs just to help make ends meet. I often said to them, "if you have extra money, spend it on my siblings." My mother knew I did not want to add to their worry, but she tried anyway.

"A person never forgets random acts of kindness especially from people he or she loves. It would stay in one's memory forever and will lead to similar acts of kindness given to either family, friends or random acquaintances," I thought to

Unknowingly

myself.

Clarice came back and sat beside me.

"My father is not coming. He is in another important meeting and he will see me at home. He even forgot to ask how my day was and how the results were?" Clarice knew beforehand that her father would not show up. She was all too familiar with this situation.

"Can I wait here with you, Desmond?"

"Yes! Sure. By the way, I talked to my folks already and they are fine. I thought they were worried, but they knew that I was avoiding their call until the results come back."

I paused for a moment and anxiously asked Clarice, "Can you tell me more about your mother?"

Clarice felt at ease with me. She started opening up.

"My mother, Diana, was a physician, an Obstetrician. She was good at it but when she had me, she decided to stop. She took care of my father and me.

Diana had a good practice but valued family life more than her work.

Diana was also an only child. Her parents were separated when she was seven years old. She grew up with a blended family. Her mother, Victoria, was devastated from the divorce. She never recovered. She died a year after the divorce.

"Diana did not expect that she would marry and have a family. She initially thought she would grow old alone. She had depression but was able to manage it with some medications and with the help of her psychiatrist. She started to be happy after getting married and begun raising a family. Once she gave birth to Clarice, she battled with postpartum depression. Depression lingered and eventually her sense of hopelessness got worse. This led to

her taking her own life." Clarice kept this thought to herself.

Clarice suddenly became quiet and tears rolled down her rosy cheeks.

"I miss her. When she died, I felt that a part of me died, too. I missed the way she would talk to me. I missed her hugs." Clarice did not reveal to me, how her mother died. This part of her story, she kept it to herself. But she shared the feelings she had that day to me. She would not share this to anyone but today she felt I am different from every-one else. She knew that I can be trusted, and I will not judge her. So, I listened to her as she opened up to me.

"My last memory of her was when she was teaching me the word "grit" - to persevere in the face of problems. The night before she died, she came in my room. She saw me struggling with my homework. She told me never to give up and to have grit. She made me promise not to forget that word. I might need it someday. The following day, she died in her sleep," Clarice did not want to tell me the whole, complete story. She suddenly began to cry inconsolably.

Clarice remembered what happened vividly in her mind. Each year she relived it and it got stronger each passing year. As I found out later, Clarice was eight years old when she found Diana hanging in the walk-in closet.

She just arrived from school and called out for her. Not hearing an answer back, she searched for her. She could not find her anywhere. Clarice finally went to her bedroom closet and found her lifeless and alone.

"Mom!" The household help and the driver came rushing in after hearing Clarice yelled.

They took Clarice away and took Diana down from where she hanged herself. That day was today. Each year had been difficult for Clarice to bear.

No one knew that Diana was desper-
ate and that it would lead to this. Everyone taught
she was happy and was beating her depression.
Everyone was wrong. That day changed everything
for Clarice and her father. The sorrow that engulfed
her mother had taken charge of their lives. It's an
uninvited feeling that did not want to go away. It's
something that you could not run away from.

Clarice never saw her father smile since that
day. As if life was sucked out of him. Mr. Landere
separated himself from life and others. He buried
himself with work and alcohol. He became emotionally numb and had forgotten Clarice - as if Clarice
died as well that day.

I was listening and never took my eyes away
from Clarice.

I tried to visualize in my mind how hard this
day would be for Clarice. I felt unbearable heavi-
ness on my chest. I felt what Clarice was feeling as
if it was my own feeling.

"As I listened to you, I know that I will never understand how hard it is to lose a mother. I would not even know what to say to someone who has that in his or her plate. I am pretty sure that you have handled it better than I would have. I know how strong you are, and I am happy for you. You honored your mother's request to never give up no matter how hard and overwhelming your situation became."

"I'm certain that your mother and father are proud of you and definitely, I am too!" I hugged her again and tears flowed from her eyes."

"Thank you, Desmond!"

Chapter 5
Memories
of Struggle

DESMOND

"Struggle is a word that I have been accustomed to. I knew everyone had their own struggles. No one is exempted. Everybody dealt with challenges or problems everyday. The difference lied on how people chose to confront their problems. Some seemed to be so happy without a care in the world. They pretend to have no problems but deep inside they are being eaten up inch by inch by their problems without them knowing it. The more you avoided your problem, the stronger it gets in controlling you.

"Some people shut down when faced with problems. Paralyzed by it, they sink into a deeper hole for themselves. The rest of us attempt to *resolve it as best as we could. Unfortunately, there is no road map cast in stone to get us out from its grasp. We learn something different each day when we try to solve it. We either search for something that could help us get out of it or we choose to stay in an abyss of despair that is left unchecked.*

"The road to happiness has always been within us. If you cannot find it, allow somebody to help you find it"

I began to open to Clarice, too, "I also had a difficult time these last few years and nobody knew about it!" I nervously conveyed to her.

"I almost did not make it to this day. My family's business had some financial problems. As a result, we struggled to pay for a lot of things including my expenses for my medical school."

"I did not know! Why didn't you come to me for help? Desmond, you know that you can ask help from me."

"Yes! I knew I can depend on you!"

"So? Why didn't you?"

"I was too proud. I am sorry!"

"We used to have enough financial resources to live comfortably and afford my medical school without any difficulty.

"The trouble began when our business failed. It was an enormous pressure to figure out how to sustain my last year of education under that situation."

"Was that the reason early this year, you barely talked to me? I was wondering why you looked so depressed then." Clarice asked.

"Yes, it all started early this year. I wanted to tell you, but I didn't have the nerve to do so."

"Oh, Desmond..."

"I remembered money was so short that I started to be late on payments for my rent. I had no funds to buy the books that I needed. Every three days, I would wash my uniforms just to carry me through the whole week. I did everything I could to save on expenses just to survive.

"There was once a day when it was too much, and I almost gave up. It was the day when my girlfriend broke up with me. My rent payment was past due for 3 months. On top of that, I was writing a promissory note that I would be paying my tuition fee in a week.

"To add insult to injury, I came home that night, and found my apartment door shut and had a lock on it. Attached to the door was a note that my belongings were sequestered. I beg the caretaker to get some of my things. He allowed me to get only two things- my duffel bag filled with books and clothes, and a twin mattress that I can sleep on. At that point I became homeless."

"Where did you stay that night?" Asked Clarice while biting her lip. She could not hide the apprehension written all over her demure face.

"I tried calling every friend I knew from my phone. Eventually someone took me in. Picture this if you can. In the middle of the night, you see a guy in white uniform carrying a twin mattress on top of his head in the middle of the road. I felt sorry for myself. I was so apprehensive about my future."

"I cannot imagine how I could have handled that situation as well as you did. I am glad some-body took you in." Clarice moved in closer to comfort me as she saw me tear up.

"I was the first child from my brood to go to college. I have three more siblings going to college soon. My parents tried their best to support all of us. Navigating the enormous cost of my medical education with my sibling's schooling is enough to strain most families especially those with financial troubles.

"I did odd jobs such as manning a copier machine. I stopped buying books, extra uniforms, and other things I needed. My meals got affected as well and I lost weight in trying to save money."

Clarice was quiet and her eyes were wide open with disbelief as she listened. She would nod at times and urged me to continue. She was a good listener.

"I remembered when I was in a fast food restaurant one day, I only had five dollars to spend for the whole day. Despite feeling sorry for myself, I shared some of what I had with the children begging for food. Though desperate for money, I shared what little I had, to complete strangers who needed it more than me.

"I can hear my parents repeatedly saying, do not forget to be kind despite having difficulties. Sharing any little thing you have will give you happiness that people can spend a lifetime trying to find."

"Your parents are proud of you, Desmond! They did a good job in raising you up!"

"Thanks, Clarice! It was really hard for them to see me struggling with money." I began to remember how hard it was for my parents to keep us financially afloat. My mind slowly wandered as I paused and stayed silent. Clarice saw how deep I was with my thoughts. She kept silent herself.

As I turned to Clarice, I resumed sharing with her what happened to me. "In my final year, I was at the end of my rope. The university was giving me an ultimatum to settle my debts or decide to miss out my final year due to nonpayment."

I did not have money and I did not know what to do. I found myself walking around this very field, deciding whether to quit or not. A familiar face recognized me. It was John, the security guard, I shared coffee with.

John was looking for me. He wanted to share some good news with me. "I have been looking for you the whole day. I remembered, the last time we talked, you were having problems with your finances. I think this person can help you!"

"Thanks, John! But with the financial problems I have right now, I think I need a miracle to come out of this mess!"

"Well, in that case, this is the miracle you have been waiting for. I was happy to find you here and I am ecstatic to tell you, I know someone who can help!"

"Who?"

"Fr. Cruz, who is currently the head of the scholarship committee. See him at the seminary as soon as you could. I already mentioned you to him. I hope everything will work out for you!"

I was pleasantly surprised. Of all the people who could help me, it was John who went out of his way to bail me out of my predicament. John did not forget a conversation we had about his and my life.

Who knew that John would remember our conversation and ended up as the only hope for me in the end.

Very early the next morning, I met with Fr. Cruz and gave him my application letter. I asked him to consider me for a year of scholarship. "I heard great things about you, Desmond, and I am happy to help you. I will present your request for financial assistance during our forthcoming meeting. By the end of the week, you will hear from me. I cannot promise you what the final decision of the committee will be, but I promise you I will do my best to convince them to approve your request."

"No worries, Father! Seeing me already means a lot to me! You already have given me hope during my desperate moment. Thank you again!"

Fr. Cruz presented my case to the committee and another doctor, Dr. Corazon Lim, immediately raised her hand. "I will take care of his request. Tell him not to worry! My only request is that he would not know who helped him. Tell him to keep passing it forward like what he did with the street children he shared his food with!"

I could hardly believe that someone would help me without expecting payment in return. I was speechless as I grasped the hand of Father Cruz tightly.

"Thank you! Please tell the committee members, I won't let you down."

Flashback of sacrifices and things I had to endure came rushing back to me. I did not expect to reach this last day. In a few more hours, it will all be done.

Clarice was amazed with my stories. She did not realize how tough the road I took just to get to this day of judgment. Like me, she also had her own struggles and crosses to bear though under different circumstances. Coincidentally, we had the same vigor and passion in trying to overcome our struggles. She felt less alone. She was so preoccupied with her sad day. She did not realize that other people like her might be struggling too.

A thought raced through my mind. *"Everyone has his or her own cross to carry. Even the strongest has his or her bad day. It is not how heavy or what your cross might be. Will you carry it as a burden, or will you take it as an opportunity to persevere and triumph?"*

Clarice squeezed my hand. "I wish I knew about the time that you were struggling. I could have helped you... you know!

"I did not want to bother you. It is my fault not to ask for your help. I was too proud and stubborn in thinking that I could solve it myself."

"It's alright! I am proud of you, Desmond on how you did it! Your simple random act of kindness had been given back to you a hundred-fold. Every good deed you throw out to the world, will boomerang back to you no matter how hard you try to ignore and avoid having it reciprocated!"

"Exactly the thoughts I had, Clarice. After I do random acts of kindness, I silently say a prayer.

"God, may I forget this kindness that I have shown. Let it not go to my head, so that tomorrow I might not remember it and do another good deed. Amen."

Chapter 6
Love

DESMOND

Clarice and I had been friends since our first year in medical school. We had gone through a lot of hardships and heartaches. We had been always there for each other when things went wrong, and life threw a curve ball.

Clarice, a tall brunette, can melt your iced heart with her warm laughter. She had both beauty and brains. You would think that she had hundreds of suitors trying to win her heart, but she had only a few. Most men were intimidated and shied away from her. Men did not want to feel inferior and thought she was too good for them. Men that she had been with were mostly unapologetic and care more for themselves. She was not lucky to find the right man. They all started with their best foot forward but showed their narcissistic true self in the end.

She once had a relationship with Jason, a rich architectural student who in the beginning showered her with attention and gifts. He would let his driver pick her up from school and take her anywhere she wanted. He took her to trips abroad during summer breaks. He seemed a pretty good match for her at the start.

Clarice eventually noticed that he does not like her to go out by herself, not even with her friends. She had to let him know when she went out of her house and when she returned home. It came to a point that it suffocated her. Clarice had to end it. Clarice still felt devastated although it was a toxic relationship. An ended relationship would mean being alone again.

Despite her breakups and heartaches, she knew how to separate her personal life from school activities. She knew her priorities very well. She made a conscious decision to let love wait for a while.

"I will deal with you later! You, sadness, have to wait because I have to do well on this exam first!"

She whispered these words to herself as she went to school with a broken heart. She learned how to be compartmentalized. Setting aside your problems to deal with other things in your life. She did not shy away from her problems. She met them head on amidst being overwhelmed with emotions of sorrow, panic and loneliness.

"Come what may! This too shall pass!" Borrowed phrases that she remembered from a movie.

We were batchmates. When we started, we had four sections; each class had at least 50 students each. We did not have a chance to know the other students because of the schedule and demands of medical school life. I met Clarice by accident.

Unknowingly

The day Clarice broke up with her boyfriend,
our paths accidentally crossed in a bridge
connecting the main school to the hospital.

Clarice was in a hurry and took the short cut
from the hospital to the covered hallway for her
Physiology class. She was holding close to her
chest several books and dropped one on the floor
as she hurriedly walked towards the end of the
covered bridge. I just ended one of my classes. I
was exiting on that very same door. I saw her drop
the book and without glancing at her, I knelt and
picked up her book. I made eye contact and unknowingly gave her the biggest smile.

"Here you go! I hope your day gets better!"

Not knowing what Clarice was going through,
those words meant a lot to Clarice. She felt a sudden warmth in her once cold lonely day. She
experienced an unexpected burst of unexplained
happiness. That moment was enough to lift Clarice
spirits up and erased her sadness completely. At
that moment when I saw Clarice and picked up her

book, I did not plan on saying that. I was really wishing her to have a better day. I got up and went my way without even realizing that unintentional encounter meant a lot for her.

Clarice went on her way too, but now has a certain glow in her once gloomy mood. A frown she had before she got to school was replaced by a smile of someone who was going to have a good day. That day was the beginning of a beautiful friendship between Clarice and me.

I had my share of relations. I had memorable relationships which would last for years.

But in the end, without the fault of no one, relationships eventually end. At times, it would be my own doing. Sometimes I would break it off to be fair. No matter how hard it would be, I would be honest about it instead of prolonging the agony.

Every relationship left a lasting impression on me. Every moment, memory, argument, and happiness became a part of me. It was my passage to become a better version of myself in moving forward to my next relationship.

I remembered one particular moment in my life when I thought I already met the one.

"Hi! I see that you are studying for an exam!" I bravely asked a stranger in a coffee shop.

I was passing by the glass window of a famous coffee shop when in the corner of my eye, I saw someone who I was attracted to. I was not able to resist going inside the coffee shop. I just have to meet her even if it could result in an awkward interaction with her. I did not know her, but I was instantly hooked with her angelic face and radiant skin complimenting her pink shirt.

So, I said to myself, "Why not? I have nothing to lose except for looking like a fool if she ignores me."

"I know you are asking yourself who I am. Honestly, we do not know each other. But I noticed you, as I was passing by and felt the urge to talk to you. I am Desmond by the way!"

She smiled and fixed her hair around her ear. Her faced turned red and felt embarrassed. She answered back.

" I am Alecx."

" I see that you are studying anatomy." Desmond pointed to her Netter's Book of anatomy.

" I just finished my exam about it!"

"Yes. I am and I do hope I'll do well."

We spoke for an hour and eventually with a leap of faith we exchanged numbers. I eventually went out with her on dates and every time I see her, I have butterflies in my stomach. Not much came out of our dates, we just became friends. I realized that Alecx's attention was spread thin with her many suitors. I felt that she would never reciprocate the way I felt for her.

Being a hopeless romantic, I decided to end it in a special way. On the actual date of her birthday, I gave her a farewell gift that she would not forget - a gift she can treasure. I made a poster out of a long white cloth. It read, "My gift is a memory! Every time you will see this spot, you will smile. Happy Birthday, Alecx!"

I hanged it around the third-floor pillars of the medical school building after classes were done. No one was there to see me put up the sign. After I set it all up, I went to her apartment. I asked her to follow me so that I could give her my gift.

Alecx was reluctant at first but she eventually agreed to follow me. It was past eight in the evening when we reached the main entrance of the building. I led her out in an opening near the middle of the building. I asked her to look up and I uttered the words written on the sign. Alecx was speechless and did not know how to respond to the surprise. I hugged her and whispered, "Happy Birthday!"

The gift left Alecx shocked. I then got the

sign for her. I neatly folded it and handed it to her. I knew this was the last time I would see her. I got her home and I never made an effort to get in touch with her again. In a way, that was my way of saying goodbye to her.

Alecx tried to reach out to me again when she realized that she had not heard from me for the longest time. But I knew that was the day that I realized that it was not meant to be. I just wanted to end it in a special way even though I knew, I would not get anything in return.

Clarice and I had our deal with on and off relationships with other people. In between those failed relationships, we remained good friends. We never crossed the line for falling for each other. We offered each other a shoulder to cry on when things did not go the way we expected.

Our platonic relationship allowed us to talk candidly and without any reservation. Every single heartbreak that we had, we dissected it objectively. Oftentimes, we did not even have to offer any advice to the other. Clarice and I were just ever present for each other. Listening until the other is done saying whatever he or she had to say.

"*Often, I could not resist expressing my opinion on every issue, but I now realized that sometimes, all we need is someone who just listens to us. Listening is a gift that is getting scarce due to the fast-pace life that we live in. Sometimes, I have such a difficult time in letting myself stand still and be silent. One should possess adaptability and unselfishness to listen attentively to someone else's problems.*

"*Eventually, I learned how to be silent and just listen. The rewards to the individual who received it is immeasurable. It satisfied the yearning to be noticed and be heard. It had the capacity to fill a void and made someone feel acknowledged. It made a person felt better about himself or herself.*"

I would seek out Clarice after each breakup I had. Clarice had always been generous with her time with me. She had shown empathy and acknowledged my sadness. I reciprocated this as well. When Clarice needed me, I would drop everything and gave her the undivided attention she needed. We would often not utter any comments or advice; we simply sat beside each other without uttering a word.

"That is the power of listening. It can make you feel better in difficult times."

"Desmond, thank you for all the times that you have listened to me. Even though you did not have to." Clarice reminisced of the numerous times we talked in the past.

"You are welcome. You had done the same for me. You're a good friend. You know, good friends like you are difficult to come by nowadays."

Clarice remembered the countless hours that we spent conversing about our struggles. During all those times, we were there for each other. She realized that giving my time to be with her filled an emptiness she had. Happiness could come out of relationships. When everything in this world is ruined and lost, relationship would remain intact. Relationships that are nurtured would last a lifetime. That was what Clarice and I had. We were more than friends. We did not even realize or say it; we were family.

"We have been through a lot and have been there for each other. I hope everything will work out especially for you, Desmond!" Clarice's eyes welled up with concern as she talked to me.

"I know it will! Though I am not certain if I will pass the final exam, I know, I gave it my all. I have no regrets, no matter what the results may be. But if it is possible, I really want to pass." I ended with a laugh.

Clarice and I had sat in front of the field for quite some time now, not realizing we had spent hours reminiscing the past. Time would pass by when you are in the company of someone you can relate with. A cloud of sorrow that followed Clarice the whole day now seemed to disappear. She felt

the heavy weight of this day being lifted. It somehow helped her move on forward with this day even
though her absent father was not around to comfort
her.

Clarice silently thought of her mother on this
day when she died.

*"I know I was young when you died mom but
in my innocent young mind, I knew and felt your
love. Amidst your despair, you were able to love
me. You somehow taught me the lesson of grit, the
best possible way you can do at that time.*

*"As if you knew that you were dying and in
your last breath, you were thinking about me. Now I
get it. This day should not be about sadness. It
should be remembered in terms of how much you
loved me and how much you were thinking about
me during your most desperate moment."*

You could see a certain aura of realization
flashing in Clarice's face. Her once gloomy eyes

were now beaming with hope and glimmering with happiness.

Chapter 7
Crossroads

CLARICE

A day prior to the final exam results reveal, I felt anxious and afraid. I had not gotten out of the house and barely had eaten. Paralyzed with grief, I spent my time alone at home.

My father has not come home since Friday night. He was eventually brought by a friend around 1:00 AM, Monday morning, drank and incoherent. His friend, Ramon, had been with him to keep him safe. He had been heavily drinking several hours before Ramon brought him home.

My father was a far cry from who he was before my mother died. He had been lost without her and had forgotten me. I reminded him of the love he had lost.

His breath reeked of alcohol and his face was moist with tears and sweat. His eyes were red, and he mumbled incomprehensible words.

"I was with him, Clarice, and I kept him safe. He had been drinking all day long!"

"Thanks for bringing him in, Ramon. Could you help me bring him in the bedroom?"

Ramon on his left and I on his right, we dragged him into a room adjacent to their master bedroom. My dad had not been sleeping in the room where they found my mom hanged in the walk-in closet.

"Thanks, Ramon!"

"Take care of him and you take care too. I must go and be with my family. Do not hesitate to call me if you need anything else."

Ramon waved goodbye and disappeared in a dark corridor.

"Rest now Dad! I hope you feel better when you wake up." I removed his shoes, covered him up with a warm blanket and left him.

As I turned the corner, I saw the master bedroom and felt the urge to go inside.

I understood my father. I, too, felt empty as I dealt with my mother's passing. And it got even worse each year as her death anniversary came closer. Coincidentally, the day when my final exam results were released was the day when my mother hanged herself.

"It is her death anniversary!"

As I entered their room, I smelled the familiar sent of lavender that my mother loved. Sheets of bedding were neatly tucked in the corners of the beds. The comb, mirror, and things she used stood still frozen in time. Nothing had changed nor moved. Though helpers cleaned the room regularly, they did not dare touch or move anything from where they were before. As I sort through my mother's belongings, I did not realize that I had been in their room for several hours now.

I finally walked into their bathroom, which led to her walk-in closet and dresser. I noticed a hand-written card in the corner of the bathroom mirror. "I love you, Mommy!" I scrawled this in red crayon when I was young.

I tried to remember my mother's face and I felt guilty of forgetting some of the details of how she looked. I began to browse and open her things. Underneath a Manila folder, I found blue envelopes with words written behind them that read, "To my dearest Angel!"

Every birthday I had, my mother gave me a birthday card. I started to sob as I held those cards close to my chest. Each year I had been finding it harder to avoid feeling sad and desperate. My mother's passing and the way I found her, left a lasting effect on me. I could not erase the image of her lifeless body hanged on a beam inside her walk-in closet. Its memory created a profound sense of helplessness, which just got stronger as her death anniversary approached.

I relived that day each time her death anniversary came near. I had done well since that day with the help of my psychiatrist. I learned how to cope and suppress it. But each passing year had proven to be more difficult to bear. Feelings of hopelessness and despair got stronger.

I had not left my house for two days now. I had barely slept and ate. I usually would shake this feeling off and refocused myself with other distractions. But today seemed to be difficult.

I had been crying as I saw my mother's things. I gathered myself and placed her birthday cards back where I found them. As I did this, I noticed a reflection of a brown image on top of my mother's dresser. I could hardly see it. All I could see was that it had several knots wrapped around it. I reached out for an old black chair, which creaked as I stepped on it.

With my outstretched arms, I reached out and grabbed the end of it. When I brought it down to get a better look at it, I suddenly felt dizzy. My vision became blurred and all I would see was near blackness. I started to hyperventilate as I realized what I had found - the rope that my mother tied on the decorative beam in her walk-in closet. It was inadvertently set aside on top of the dresser when they brought my mother down from the beam. Nobody had removed it. It had been forgotten all these years.

I cried uncontrollably and felt a heavy pressure on my chest. I held the rope so tight that I felt like my fingernails where tearing the skin out of my palm.

"Why did you leave me Mom? Is it my fault?" I said these words to myself with a cracked voice.

My feelings started to swell and became

unbearable. My dad was passed out and was not there to comfort me in my most vulnerable moment. The door was shut, and I was alone.

I was down on my knees, whispering to myself.

"I do not have much to live for anyway. I am tired of this pain of losing you, Mom!"

Tears kept rolling down my cheeks. I looked up and realized what I must do. I got up again on the black chair which was now directly underneath the beam where my mom was before. In a moment of weakness, I tied the rope around the beam and secured it.

I thought of hanging myself like how my mother, Diana, did it. I held onto the rope tightly with both hands now. I started widening the gap in between it to insert my head. My eyes were now shut, and I was mumbling incomprehensible words to myself as I felt the rope tightly wrapped around my neck.

"Ping! Ping! Ping!"

"Ping! Ping! Ping!"

"Ping! Ping! Ping!" So alerted my cellphone of received messages. I initially did not hear it and I positioned myself in order to jump forward.

"I will see you soon, Mom!"

But my phone would not let up, It caught my attention now. Unexpectedly, I stopped what I was about to do and came back to my senses. I was caught off guard. I wondered who wanted to get in touch with me this early. I loosened the noose of the rope and dropped on the floor on a fetal position crying inconsolably.

"Ping!"

Alerted my phone of unchecked messages. Sobbing still, I reached out for it. It was Desmond who had sent me messages!

"Today is D-Day! I hope you are already up. Good luck to us!"

"Good luck today! I know you will do well!"

"I will be praying for us! I will see you in school."

I looked at the time and it was already 5:25 in the morning. I was about to end it all. For an unexplained reason, the alerts caused by Desmond's messages had stopped me from doing so.

I left the rope hanging.

"What is one more day to delay it from happening!"

"Memories of my mother came rushing in. The day before she passed, my mom talked to me about lessons of persevering and not giving up. To have grit in everything, no matter how hopeless they might seem. All these years, I tried honoring my promise to never forget those lessons and to

live by them every day of my life.

"In the moment of utmost desperation, pick yourself up and move on" Those were the last words I remembered my mom saying to me.

"Clarice, always remember to persevere and to have grit!"

With this thought, I reluctantly picked myself up and compartmentalized how I felt.

I realized that if my phone did not interrupt me, I could have ended my life right there and then. Desmond unexpectedly saved me.

"Maybe I should think things through and see what happens today," I said this to myself as I prepared to go to the university and meet up with Desmond.

Desmond will not know how important his role was in putting a hold on my plans. He unknowingly helped me come to my senses and prevented a tragic loss of life.

I stepped out, boarded my white SUV and headed for school. This was about the same time that Desmond was heading down from his apartment and started walking towards our university. We saw each other on the second floor of the medical building and had talked about me passing the exam with honors and that Desmond had to wait, since the remaining list of students will not be released until the final deliberations by the faculty.

I kept everything to myself. I did not have the courage to tell him what happened to me earlier. We parted ways eventually and met again in front of the field. This second meeting provided the unexpected support we both needed.

It is almost three in the afternoon when we heard an alert on Desmond's phone.

"Ping! Ping! Ping!"

Unknowingly

"Final exam results are in!"

Chapter 8
Unknowingly

DESMOND

As Clarice and I got up from our bench, several students with white uniforms stood up in unison. They all received the message that the results were in. The faculty just finished their deliberations and posted the list of students who passed. Not seeing your name on the list would mean a repeat of a year in medical school.

One could hear the incomprehensible chatter from students as they rushed to the announcement bulletin board in the main building. Everyone felt the tension and anxiety of not being on the list. We had waited for this day. In a few minutes, each one will know if he or she could move onto the next step in becoming a full-fledged physician.

"Do you mind me coming with you, Desmond?" Asked Clarice.

"Not at all. No matter what the results may be, I want you to be there. No regrets! I did everything I could."

Clarice and I were engulfed by a crowd of slowly moving students passing through the narrow corridors of the main lobby. I remembered the first time I passed through these corridors. I was filled with excitement and eagerness to get started. I saw the long wooden chairs where I spent unaccounted number of hours in studying and waited for classes to start. I smelled the familiar soothing scent of fresh flowers placed each morning underneath an altar of the Blessed Virgin Mary in the hallway as I proceeded to my classes. I saw the faces of familiar librarians with whom I shared a laugh or two in the past.

"Here goes nothing!" I whispered to myself.

We started to ascend the stairs to reach the announcement board. I soon reached the second floor with Clarice. A large group of students had taken every space available in the long hallway near the Dean's office.

"Everyone is still waiting! Do you know if they already posted the list of names?" Clarice asked a classmate as she tapped her shoulder

"No. Not yet, but the Dean's secretary just came out a while ago and announced that they are done with the list of students who passed."

Suddenly, everybody was silent. I heard a door unlocked and turned my head towards the direction. A petite young lady wearing a blue suit emerged from the door. On her left hand, was a brown folder. Everyone was following her movements and she somehow forced a smile. She was quite overwhelmed with the sheer volume of students waiting. She felt self-conscious but she calmly removed a stock of papers out of the folder.

She pulled four papers with white covers in front of them. Underneath it, was the list of students who passed. Nobody dared to interrupt her or ask any question. We all held our breaths as she removed the cover of the lists. She opened the glass window and individually pinned each paper on the corked bulletin board. When she was done, there were a few seconds that passed before someone dared to be the first one to look for their name. The first batch of students to check their names was like a bottleneck of cars you would see in a traffic jam. They jostled each other to be in a better position to view the list.

"I passed!" Shouted one of my friends.

Everyone clapped. Amidst that celebration you saw serious faces as they left the announcement board. Most would turn a hidden corner and avoid the cheering crowd. Tears rolled down from their cheeks as they realized, their names were not among the passers. Others were on their phones, sharing the good news with their loved ones and parents, with loud voices and without a care in the world. In the mixture of happiness and sadness, I turned to Clarice.

"I will look now. Can you stay here for a bit and I will be right back."

Clarice nodded. "Good luck, Desmond!" She reached for my hand and grasped it tightly. I smiled back at her as I squeezed her hand too.

"Everything will be fine!"

I weaved through the crowd and waited for my turn to be in front of the board. Inching my way in, I finally reached the front. I scanned through the alphabetical list of students in section A. I reached the second column and my hand started to shake as I saw the surnames which started with an E. I started to worry and decided to browse through it again. On the bottom of the first column I saw it.

"18. Desmond E. Dinaire!"

I could not remember the last time I was so

happy reading my name. I slowly exhaled and felt a heavy weight lifted from my shoulders. The wait is over; I have finally done it. I passed! As I turned towards Clarice with a wide grin on my face, my classmates started to congratulate me.

"We made it!" A classmate said to me as I squeezed out of the crowd. I said thank you and started to walk towards the direction where Clarice was. Amidst the chaos of laughter, I silently thanked God.

"Before I forget, thank you God for everything! Without you, none of these would be possible."

I passed through familiar faces with eyes lit with utmost joy. I reached a point where the crowd thinned out and caught a glimpse of Clarice's face. She was quiet and held her hands in front of her. Once she got a glimpse of me with my head down, in between two students, she stood still in anticipation. I walked faster but was interrupted by a herd of cheering students, who obscured my line of sight of her.

Clarice searched for me, but I had been covered by a huge crowd. I lost sight of her. I decided to go in a hallway around the crowd. I reached the other side and I saw Clarice's back turned away from me. She was finally in front of me as I reached to tap her shoulders. Clarice turned towards me and my face was emotionless at first. But I then started to grin, and I gave out a big smile. Clarice lunged herself to me and embraced me with pure joy. I hugged her back. I never felt so happy to be with someone hugging me like the way she did.

Clarice and I stayed motionless for a minute drowning the celebratory noise around us with our moment.

"I passed Clarice! I made it! I said softly near Clarice's ear.

I had tears in my eyes as I released my tight squeeze on Clarice. She saw the tears rolling down my cheeks.

"I am so happy to be here with you. All your hard work paid off in the end. Never did I see you cry like this. I feel fortunate to see you so happy."

Clarice and I then turned toward the stairs and reached the pavilion in front of the building where her father usually waited for her.

"Did your father call you back on what time he will meet up with you?"

"Yes he did! He said he might be late and instead he will see me when I get home."

"Where to now?" Asked Clarice as she attempted to change the topic.

"How about you? What plans do you have after this?"

Before I was able to answer back my phone

rang. I excused myself for a minute to talk to my dad.

From a distance Clarice saw me beaming with happiness as I relayed the news to my parents. Though Clarice felt joy for me, she dreaded the thought of going home. She left her house in a hurry. She noticed that the car of her father had already gone when she left the house. Her father always tried to avoid this day and numbed himself with alcohol to lessen the pain of losing her mom. Clarice slowly gazed down the floor and wondered how she will confront what nearly happened this morning.

"Sorry Clarice. That was my dad. I just told them that I passed, and they were so happy for me! As I walked towards her, I saw her with a blank stare and with a worried look on her face. There was a frown where a smile used to be.

"Is everything OK? You suddenly looked serious and in deep thought."

"I just feel tired. I hardly slept last night! I will be fine after I get some rest tonight," answered Clarice as she tried to hide from me what she truly felt. I sensed that she somewhat felt embarrassed that I noticed it. She did not want to drown down the happiness that I was having. She forced herself to change her mood.

Clarice forced a smile and asked, "What plans do you have after this? Any celebration?"

"I will head home and catch the last bus tonight, to be with my parents and siblings. I already packed and I am just waiting for the last bus schedule."

I sat beside Clarice on the cement benches near the end of the long pavilion. Clarice looked me in the eye and said, "I am happy for you. All your prayers have been answered. Seeing you happy, really makes me happy."

"Sorry for the times I pestered you with sad stories of frustration. Thank you, Clarice. Without you, I probably would not have survived medical school."

Clarice was surprised at what I just said. "I did not know that I had helped you."

"Yes, you did! The countless hours you spent listening to me, helped me a lot. You were there for me. It meant a lot to me more than you can imagine."

"You have been an inspiration to me too, Desmond! All the sacrifices that you have endured are not easily handled. Some people would have quit if they were in your shoes. You persevered through times that seemed hopeless. You taught me to have faith in myself for eventually I will reach the finish line. If you had to crawl to get there, so be it. Sooner or later, I will get the goals I had in the beginning no matter how hard the situation might seem."

"Ooohh! That is so nice of you to say, Clarice. Not too many people know me the way you described it. Thanks for being there until the end. You have helped me get through my hard times and saved me from quitting."

Suddenly I saw Clarice well up with tears again.

"What is wrong? Did I upset you?

"No! I am just so happy for you. These are tears of joy!"

She remembered how her day started. She did not tell me that I unknowingly saved her life.

Chapter 9
Surrendering to
a Higher Power

CLARICE

It was about five in the afternoon and the last bus was scheduled to leave at six. The crowd of students had gone, and just a few remained. There were only a few cars passing by to pick up students. The Pavilion was almost empty, except for me, Desmond and a pair of students who were on the other side of it. Though I wished not to go home yet, I checked on my watch and thought I should let him go. So, I made an excuse even though I still wanted to be with him.

"I better head home. My dad might be waiting for me?" I reluctantly said these words although I believed that my dad won't be there.

"I better go too. I might miss my bus going home. This day is special. I am glad I was able to spend it with you, Clarice."

We both did not want to leave each other's side, but we hesitantly stood up at the same time. We began walking towards my SUV, which was parked a few yards from where we sat.

"You take care going home!"

"You, too, Desmond."

Desmond leaned over and kissed me on my cheek for the first time.

"Bye! I will see you when I see you." Desmond smiled as he waved goodbye to me.

"Goodbye, Desmond!" I waved back at him.

I started my car and headed home. Along the way, I thought of my mom.

"This is for you Mom. I kept my promise to you to persevere. But every year gets harder knowing you are not here. I terribly miss you!"

I tried to call my dad through my car phone, but it directly went to his voicemail. I tried calling home but to no avail. I reached the last intersection before turning into my gated subdivision. I was about to turn, but the traffic light switched back to a red light.

I recalled my mother doing something special for me every time I do good in school. I was certain, if my mom were alive, she would surprise me with a party when I got home.

"I hope I make you proud every day, Mom."

The light turned green and a car behind me was driving 60 miles per hour on a 35-mile limit road. He weaved through cars and was 200 yards away from my SUV, which I signaled to turn. I was distracted and did not see him.

He was now close to me and tried to cut into my lane.

Beep! Beep! Beep!

The driver frantically blew his horn on me. It was almost too late when I saw him, and I was fortunate to turn my wheels to the right. I almost hit the guardrails if not for my quick reflex of stepping on my brakes in time for my SUV to stop.

Through the window, I could see him gesturing with his hands and said not so nice things about me. Though I could not hear him, I could tell that he was cursing and irritated. Although I knew it was not my fault, I waved at him with an apologetic gesture. He sped passed me as I prepared to merge into traffic again.

"That was a close one!" I said to myself as I signaled to incoming traffic and got back to 100 West Road, 100 yards away from our gated subdivision.

I punched my code in the gate and it swung open. Neighbors saw me come in and waved at me. I was so preoccupied with my thoughts. In my mind all I saw was our house, which I felt was empty at this moment. No one to go home to and share what happened to me in school today.

Out of sadness and grief, I tried to talk to my mom as if she was sitting beside me.

"Why did you leave me, Mom? Now I do not have anyone to share these moments with."

"It is not fair!"

I now turn into our circular driveway and a sense of gloom overwhelmed me. It snapped away the little joy I had with Desmond. I stepped out of the SUV, not realizing that I left my keys in the ignition switch.

"Today, my father arranges for our driver and hired help to go home to their families."

He did not want them to see us wallow in grief. I reached out for the black metallic handle of our front door. It felt cold and heavy to pull open. I walked into an empty house. My dad was not home. I am not sure if he was at work or out again drinking with his friends. My phone did not have any return calls or messages from him.

I started to hyperventilate and tremble as I remembered what I had said this morning before I left for school.

"This too can wait!"

Now, I did not have a choice. I had to confront my fear, which I had set aside before. I gathered some courage to let myself inside my mom's room again. As I looked up, the tied rope was still there where I left it. The old black chair was underneath it. No one was there to alert anyone nor prevent me from doing what I attempted to do before. I sat down underneath the tied rope as I tried talk to my mom.

"I wish you were here, Mom! I feel at times I cannot do this on my own. I hope you are proud of me."

"I am tired of hurting like this and I wish it to end."

I looked at the rope dangling above me. I saw now, how my mom loosely made a knot to accommodate her head.

I mustered enough courage to stand up on the chair, which creaked as I put my weight on it. I held the rope with both of my hands as I mumbled some words.

"I love you, Mommy!"

I started tightening my grip on it and rotated it on my hand. I began to untie it from the decorative beam. I brought it down with me and placed the black chair to where I found it before.

"I am tired of this pain. I am tired of

remembering you like this. I forgive you for leaving me behind. I forgive you for not letting me say goodbye to you. I do not know what comes next after this. I accept that you are not physically here, but I know you have always been with me since a part of you exist in me. I will keep my promise to you... to be the best version of myself.

"Throughout these years I have been remembering you with pain, today I will change that. I will remember you by how you wanted me to succeed and persevere beyond my weaknesses. This is how I will remember you! I never lost you! You will always be with me. I love you, Ma and I forgive you!"

I left my mom's walk-in closet and shut the door. My breathing was better, and I felt a sudden calm which I did not have this morning. I felt sadness, but it was much tolerable now. I returned to my room. I did not realize that I left my television still on.

I sat down on the edge of my bed in front of the television. I glanced at it and noticed Keanu

Reeves' interview with Stephen Colbert was being replayed in E! News.

"What do you think what happens to us when we die, Keanu Reeves?"

Keanu Reeves paused and answered back.

"I know that the ones who loved us will miss us."

Stephen Colbert was speechless and simply shook his hand.

"Yes, I agree Keanu! I really do miss my mom!"

I finally untied the knot that my mom made. I carefully rolled the rope into an oval shape figure. Holding it with my left hand, I reached for a wooden music box on my dresser. I pulled out a red ribbon that I kept through these years. I wore it the day my mom died. I secured the rope with my hand as I tied the red ribbon around it.

I tried to call my dad, but the call went to his voicemail again. I left him a message.

"I love you, Dad! I am already at home and I am about to get out for a while; but I'll be right back. When you come back, we need to talk! See you later, Dad."

I walked back to my mother's room and I took the note that I made for her when I was 8 years old, off the mirror. I inserted it in between the rope as I then went out of the house.

I remembered I had left my keys in the car. I drove out towards the west part of the city. It was getting dark, but I saw the remaining visible orange rays of sunset. Guided by my GPS, I reached my destination. I passed through the entrance of the cemetery where my mother was laid to rest.

I walked towards her tombstone. I was shocked to see my father sitting beside her grave.

I was able to muster some words, "I am glad

that you are with Mom today, Dad!"

My dad was surprised to hear my voice and hugged me without uttering a response. He was sober and was with her the whole day. He had dried tears on his face.

"What are you doing here, Clarice?"

"I found this rope above her dresser."

My dad was in disbelief that it was all along inside their room. He had a worried look on his face. How unimaginable could it have been for her daughter to find it and recognized this rope. Seeing my dad's reaction, I reassured him.

"I am OK with it now. I have already forgiven Mommy for leaving me and you should forgive her too!"
As soon as I finished my words, he pulled me close to him and cried on my shoulder.

"I am so sorry that I have not been with you

all these years. I was lost without your mom"

" It's OK, Dad. I forgive and love you!"

"I love you too, Clarice!"

Together we stood in front of the tombstone that read, "Diana Landere, a loving Mother and Wife."

We both knelt down and buried the rope beside her tomb with the note inserted in between it.

"I love you, Mommy!"

"I will never forget you. You will always be with us. I hope I make you proud every day!" I pressed my fingers on my lips and gave her a flying kiss goodbye.

"I'll see you later, Mom!"

I turned to my father.

"Let's go home, Dad!" My dad nodded in agreement and held my hand as we both waved goodbye to her.

Unknowingly

Chapter 10
Forgiveness

CLARICE

My dad decided to ride with me leaving his car behind. As he drove for me, I noticed my father looked at peace. His demeanor had changed. His once stiff posture turned into a more relaxed state of mind as he weaved through traffic. His wrinkled, worried facial expression had now been changed into his old self - smiling in contentment. As my dad held the steering wheel, it brought back happy memories of the days when I was younger, when laughter and stories dominated car rides. My mother might had passed but we both felt her presence with us.

"Maybe there is still hope for him. He had suffered long enough. He deserves a shot to be happy." I pondered while I stared at my dad.

"Sorry Clarice if I have neglected you all these years. I made a mistake!"

"What mistake, Dad?"

"I have been absent in your life for a long while now. I do not want to continue that mistake. I am glad that I am with you now."

"I am, too. I wanted to tell you that I passed and will graduate with honors."

"Wow!" My dad's eyes widened with a sudden pause in his breathing. He quickly realized that he had missed a lot with what was going on with my life. He vowed that he would turn things around and that he would be a better father to me.

"If your mom were here now, we will be

having a party at home for you!" He turned the car towards Sunset Boulevard.

"May I take you out Clarice and have a date with you tonight?"

"Of course, Dad. I thought you would never ask." We both laughed and felt happy with each other's company. We ate out in a local restaurant and spent a good part of the night talking about my mother and how my day was. My father did not ask me about what really happened when I found the rope. He wanted me to tell him when I felt ready to share. It had been a long time since I felt contented and happy like this. I finally felt I could talk to my dad.

I got my father back!

We reached home, and we were just about to settle in and rest. I initially hesitated to discuss that I almost took my life this morning.

"Tok, Tok! Tok, Tok!"

"Can I come in, Clarice?"

"Door is open, Dad. You may come in," I replied as I get ready to go to bed.

Upon entering my room, my dad saw me climbed up into my bed. He saw the comforter folded near the end of my bed. He grabbed it and tried to tuck me in.

"Dad, you don't have to do that! I am 24 years old now and not a baby anymore."

"I know. I know. I just missed doing it! For me, you will always be my little princess, no matter how old you get! I just wanted to say good night and thank you!"

"Thank you? For what?"

"Thanks for bringing me back to my old self. I never thought that I could feel this way again. I feel me again. I still miss your mom, but I realized that I should not forget the people around me who love me as well. You are the reason why I feel this way. That is why I am thanking you!"

"You are welcome, Dad! I am glad you somehow feel better now. I am glad you are back!" My dad gave me a goodnight kiss on my forehead and was about to stand up to leave.

"Dad!" I yelled as I tried to hold my dad back down to sit on the bed.

"Yes, Clarice?" He paused and sat down again at the edge of the bed.

"I almost took my life this morning. I did not want to tell you at first, but I figured I had to tell you and be honest about it!"

"I am not going to judge you for what you did. We did have a hard time when your mom died but we still have each other, especially now. I would rather you not do it again. I will be lost without you!"

"I am good now and I do not think I can do that again. I remembered mom's words and a friend of mine unknowingly helped me come to my senses. My phone kept on alerting because of his messages. Desmond interrupted me at the right time without him knowing about it."

"I am glad to hear that! To tell you the truth, between us two, I think you are the stronger one. You brought me back and I will be right here with you from now on.

"I am not going anywhere, Clarice. I will be here for you. And I am proud of you. Despite the odds stocked against you, you manage to go beyond your problems. You became the best version of yourself. Your mom is proud of you, too!"

"Thanks, Dad. Nothing to worry about now. Let us start all over again!"

"Good!"

"Maybe you should invite Desmond to have dinner with us one of these days. I would like to meet him."

"I'll call him in the morning. Thanks, Dad. Love you!"

"I love you, too, princess! Get some sleep! Good night."

"Good night." My dad left and closed the door behind him.

I woke with a renewed spirit. My eyes adjusted to the beam of stray sunlight that pierced through the middle of my curtains. The sheets felt comfortable and I recognized the smell of fresh linens that were just recently changed. I slept most of the morning. The smell of fresh coffee and burnt toast filled the air.

"It had been awhile since I had this kind of sleep." I rolled to my side and sat on my bed for a minute or two. I peeked through my door and I saw

my dad was busy in the kitchen preparing breakfast for us. He caught a glimpse of me peeking through my door.

"Good morning, princess! Made some breakfast for us! Come out when you are ready."

"Alright, Dad, be out in a bit."

My dad and I spent most of the day together. He cancelled his appointments and decided to stay home with me.

"Did you call Desmond yet? I would like to meet him."

"Let me text him first to see if he is not busy. He might be doing something with his family."

Chapter 11
Separate
ways

DESMOND

I was able to catch the last bus going home. Although I was excited to go home and see my parents, I was still thinking of Clarice.

"I hope you got home safe," I was about to text her, but I hesitated. I did not want to bother her anymore.

I had been on the road for almost an hour and the bus was packed. I was able to get an aisle seat and placed my duffel bag underneath it.

Most of the passengers just got off from work and travelled home via bus. A good number of them

though not acquainted travel quite frequently together on the same bus schedules. You could hear
the chatter from passengers while they talked with
the passenger seated next to them. I was seated
with an old man who snored the moment he sat
down. He even almost laid his head on my shoulder, but I gently pushed his head towards the
backrest so that he could rest without being dis-
turbed.

"Ho-hum!" With a wide-open mouth, I suddenly made a big sleepy yawn. I dozed off even before the bus entered the freeway.

The bus made a screeching sound as the
driver pressed on its heavy brakes. We had
reached the tollgate prior to entering my town. The
driver handed a couple of paper bills to the young
lady inside the tollbooth. She gave him the biggest
smile though she had probably seen a million cars
that day.

"It's good to be home!"

Most of the passengers except for a handful, dozed off as well. The bus started to move again and turned right, eastward bound. It entered a vibrant town where I grew up. I had ridden such a bus probably a thousand times since I started medical school several years ago.

"I am home!" I whispered to myself as I smiled while seeing familiar places.

I saw the run-down restaurant whereas a kid, I would get take-outs for my family. There was the old theater, where I watched my first movie and a donut shop near the bus stop, where I usually get off. The bus slowed down and signaled for it to stop. I grabbed my duffel bag and headed toward the exit in front. On my way out, I saw through the bus window a group of people with signs on top of their heads.

I stepped down from the bus to loud cheers from a small crowd gathered in front of the bus stop.

"Yahoo! Congrats, Desmond! You did it!" Shouted a childhood friend.

"Don't forget about us!" Yelled another friend.

"Congratulations Desmond," read a poster held by my siblings. My parents organized a small crowd to welcome me home. It was rare for someone in my community to do what I had achieved. I felt like a conquering hero as I shook the hands of my friends. I thanked them for being there. Everyone was so excited for me. At the end of the small crowd were my parents with opened arms. I hugged them back and embraced my siblings, too. We crossed the street together as they were chanting my name.

My mother prepared a party for me while my father called my friends to set up the surprise for me. We sang karaoke songs all night long without a care in the world. Amidst the happy cheers and singing, my parents and I sat at the head table talking.

"We are really proud of you and never doubted you for a minute."

"Thanks Mom and Dad, for this surprise party!"

"You are welcome. You deserve it. We are just so happy for you!"

The next day, I woke up to the fresh smell of brewed coffee. My dad made coffee using a metal strainer that sat on top of a pan of boiling water. My mother fried sweet cured pork with some native eggs. My favorite breakfast. We sat around the kitchen nook as my father poured fresh coffee in my cup.

"Oh! By the way, this came from the mail for you this morning." My dad handed me a white envelope with an official seal from the Department of State, USA."

Inside that envelope was the answer to an application I had filled with an agency connected with a Johns Hopkins-affiliated hospital based in Maryland, USA, three years ago.

Prior to medical school, I worked as a nurse and decided to go to medical school. I had to take some additional courses, but I was able to get in easily. I anticipated that my family would have financial hardship in the future. I took a chance and applied in an open position as nurse in a different country where the pay was ten times more.

"This is it! I have been waiting for this for a long time now!"

"Ping, Ping!" I heard a familiar sound while I opened the letter. Clarice just sent a text message asking me if I got home safe and how my family was taking the news. I set aside my phone for a while and focused my attention on the letter.

"...NVC received your approved immigrant visa petition from USCIS." I have been approved as an immigrant to work for a hospital where I applied for, three years ago. Within a month of processing requirements, I should leave for the United States of America and start working in an American-based hospital to honor my contract.

"I did not expect that I have to leave so soon!" I said to my parents while I read the rest of the letter.

My parents welled up with sadness as they realized that after a month, I will be living far away from them. My dad placed his hand on my shoulder.

"This could be a sign of better things for you son. We are so happy for you!"

"Thanks Dad!" My siblings came in and over-heard the conversation. They started hugging me, too.

I remembered Clarice's message and I texted her back.

"Got home safe and came home to a party set up by my parents. Hope you guys had fun as well. Everything OK?"

"Yeah! My dad took me out last night for a date. LOL. He asked about you. If you are around here next week, we would be happy for you to join us for dinner."

"I'll be there next week. I will be fixing some applications. Maybe Monday?"

"Perfect! We will see you next week then. Congrats again!"

"Thanks! Congrats to you too! I'll see you next week!"

I was surprised with Clarice's request. I did not expect to be invited for dinner with her and her dad. I had mixed feelings of happiness and sadness. I was happy that everything I planned for was coming true and at the same time, sad that I will soon be leaving my family and Clarice.

I felt sudden sadness as I thought of breaking the news to Clarice. After a month, I had to leave her, and I would be far away from her.

After spending a few days with my folks, I traveled back to the inner city where the US embassy was. I stayed there for a week to finish my application, immigration documents, and at the same time meet up with Clarice. The night before I went, I texted Clarice.

"I will be there tomorrow. Where do you want to meet up?"

"I can get you if you want. Just tell me where."

"No, I'll be the one to come to you. Around 5:30 PM?"

"Yup! Are you sure you can come to our house?"

"Yeah! Just text me the address and I'll be there."

Clarice gave her address and prepared for tomorrow's dinner date. She told her dad, too. Mr. Landere instructed their personal chef to plan for a feast. He brought out his favorite wine and instructed their help to prepare the dining hall for tomorrow.

I arrived early near the address given by Clarice. It was a gated subdivision where security was tight. No one got in or out without being checked extensively up front by the attendants.

As my taxi yielded in front of the gate, the guard asked.

"May I have your name, Sir?"

"Desmond Dinaire. I am here to see Clarice Landere."

"We have been expecting you. Mr. Landere gave us clear instructions the moment you arrive!" The guard talked to the taxi driver and paid the fee for my ride. Another guard opened the door for me.

"We will take it from here." The guard motioned for the service cart to come nearer. Escorted by two guards, I noticed the palatial houses that adorned the street where Mr. Landere's house was. In front of one of the houses, I could see a figure resembling Clarice.

They already called in that I arrived. Mr. Landere and Clarice were already waiting for me.

"Thank you, officers, for helping Desmond!"

I was stepping out of the service cart when I saw the outstretched hand of Mr Landere. I grabbed it and shook his hand firmly. He pulled me in and to my surprise he welcomed me with a bear hug.

"Good evening, Sir!" Greeting him with a confused face. I did not expect such a greeting from someone who did not say much to me before. Clarice blushed with embarrassment upon seeing my reaction.

"Dad, you are squeezing him too hard."

"Oh, Sorry! I am just so happy to see him and wanted to thank him."

"Thank me, Sir?" Clarice looked at his father while gently shaking her head from side to side without me knowing.

"Oh, I just wanted to thank you for being a true friend and keeping my daughter company when I was not able to."

"Ah...You are welcome, Sir!" Clarice's face now is as red as her shirt.

We walked through a path filled with white orchids and boxwoods. We then entered a heavy double metal door. In front were servants lined up, to greet us as we proceeded to the dining hall. The house was intimidating but it took no time for me to be at ease. Mr. Landere and Clarice treated me like family.

The dinner was superb with lobsters and assortment of freshly caught seafood. We drank wine to celebrate us, for passing the final exams.

I had never seen Mr. Landere laughed so hard. I was happy to be proven wrong to think that he was a snub and aloof.

He raised his wine glass up in the air, "To two of my favorite people in the world! Finishing Med school with flying colors."

"Thank you!"

"If you can excuse me. I must attend to some unfinished business with some worried clients. I will leave you two. It has been a pleasure, Desmond. Don't be a stranger. You are welcome here anytime!"

Mr. Landere left the two of us together still drinking Meiomi, a Pinot Noir.

"This wine tastes great!"

"Yes, it tastes really good. It is an inexpensive, common wine but Dad loves it and orders boxes of it every month."

Clarice led me to the garden adjacent to the dining room while she held our glasses. As I followed her to the garden, I rubbed my nape from side to side, worried of how Clarice would react to my news. We sat down in the middle of a Japanese-themed garden near a pagoda structure.

"Clarice, I need to tell you something?"

She paused and stopped sipping her wine and asked, "What is it? You know you can tell me anything."

"There is no better way to say this, but I got approval to work abroad. I just got the letter last week and I will be leaving for the U.S., two weeks from today."

I can see Clarice's face turned serious as I broke the news to her. She placed her glass on a wooden table beside her and paused for a minute before saying a word. I held my breath until she spoke.

"I am happy for you, Desmond! Now you can support your family the way you wanted to. They need you now more than ever." Clarice replied.

Clarice saw me looking away trying to avoid eye contact. She saw my sad face as I told her that I was leaving her. She pretended to be happy for me, but it was tearing her apart.

"I will really miss you." As Clarice kept this feeling to herself.

I gathered enough courage to make eye contact with Clarice. "Thanks! Please do not forget me? OK?"

"What I really wanted to say was I really do not want to leave you and I will terribly miss you."

I held my words. Being physically far apart will not work anyway. We will only end up hurting each other more. I want her last memory of me to be pleasant and not falling apart because of the distance between us.

"Of course not! Do not forget me too, Desmond?

"I won't!"

I spent the whole night with her reminiscing our medical school days until the wee hours of the morning. We enjoyed each other's company. We both knew that it would be our last time together.

Days turned into weeks and finally the day came for me to say goodbye. My parents rented a van for the road trip we had to take to get to the airport, which was two and a half hours away from where we live.

"Goodbye, Mom and Dad! I'll see you in a year. I will try to come home next year." With a heavy heart, they let me go. I pulled my baggage onto the conveyer belt and headed to the airport security terminal.

It was 5:20 in the morning and I knew that Clarice was still asleep. I pulled out my phone and recorded a voice message for her.

"I am about to board my plane and I will be turning off my phone soon. I just wanted to say I will miss you and I hope to see you when I come back. Thank you for everything. Take care!" I turned my phone off and showed my ticket to the airport attendant prior to boarding.

Upon waking up, Clarice saw the unopened voice message on her phone. She sobbed as she heard me saying goodbye.

I arrived a quarter past ten in the morning in the East Coast. A different time zone as compared to back home.

"So, this is the feeling of being born again. No home you can call your own. No car that can take you anywhere you like. No friends or family that you can depend on when you need help with something."

I literally learned everything from scratch. Brick by brick, I tried building a life here. I worked three nights each week as a nurse. And in between shifts, I was studying for the U.S. Medical Licensing Exam (USMLE). Countless hours of externship, bedside rounds, and PowerPoint presentations.

Finally, a chance presented itself. Prayers have been answered. One resident from an Internal Medicine program suddenly quit without stating a reason why. A vacancy that needed to be filled.

"I have five more candidates that I am looking at, but I wanted to hear your thoughts first! Do you want to fill the vacant spot and start working as a doctor again?" Asked an Internal Medicine Program Director.

Without any hesitation, I emailed back and replied, "When do I start?"

I withdrew from the matching program for residents and began my training. A few minutes before I start my shift as a doctor, I say a little prayer.

"Thank you for everything, God! I will start my shift in a few minutes, may I help somebody today. If I will be a blessing to someone sick, may I forget the good things that I have done today so that tomorrow, I may do it with the same passion as if I were doing it for the first time."

I am now in my senior year in my Internal Medicine residency. Throughout the three years, Clarice and I would regularly exchange emails and phone calls. But because of the distance and the time difference between us, we struggled to stay in touch constantly.

Routine has been my friend. Every morning, I passed by my favorite local coffee shop to get a cup of coffee before I go to work.

"Hi! Good morning, Joe." I became friends with the owner of a local coffee shop, as he saw me coming in regularly.

"I'll have the usual - one tall caramel macchiato to go, Joe!"

As I sipped my coffee, I caught a glimpse of a figure in the corner of the shop. Her head was turned away from me as I saw a familiar scunci that held her hair so beautifully. I got closer to get a better look. My heart started thumping and I consciously felt each breath I was taking. The woman eventually turned her head towards me. She saw me like I was frozen in time. Our eyes met.

The woman was Clarice.

The End

Unknowingly